Firebug

by

Eric Brown

First published in Great Britain by Barrington Stoke Ltd
10 Belford Terrace, Edinburgh EH4 3DQ
Copyright © 2003 Eric Brown

The moral right of the author has been asserted in
accordance with the Copyright, Designs and
Patents Act 1988
ISBN 1-84299-103-5
Printed by Polestar AUP Aberdeen Ltd

A Note from the Author

I wanted to write a story about a boy who set fire to things. He did the wrong thing for the right reasons – or he thought they were the right reasons at the time.

I had all the story plotted out in my head, except the start. I knew what the middle would be, and I knew the ending. But what about the beginning?

Then I met a friend in the village. He asked me what I was working on, and I told him about *Firebug.*

His eyes lit up. He told me that he had set fire to someone else's bonfire when he was a boy. A friend of his had held up a match and said, "One match is all it would take".

One match …

And suddenly I knew that I had the start of my story. Thanks, Winston!

To Micklethwaite,
my pal

Contents

Chapter 1
One Match

One match ...

That was all it took. One match changed my life.

It all started on that Saturday afternoon. There was nothing on TV and I was bored with my computer games. I decided to go out.

Dad was in the kitchen, cooking one of his big dinners. "We're having some friends round tonight, Danny. I'll fix you something that you can eat in your room, OK?"

I just shrugged and went out. Every Saturday it was the same. Mum and Dad would cook for their friends. I'd be given a tray and told to eat in my room. They'd never wanted to have me anyway. They just planned the one, and that was my brother Billy.

I walked through town to the playing fields. It was an icy cold day in late October, and I could smell fireworks in the air.

Ever since leaving Halifax and coming to Barnsley, I'd been unhappy. I was starting my last year at school and I couldn't wait to leave. I had no friends here and I hated my new school.

Even worse, a lad called Ross Davis had started bullying me. I was the new boy, and I was small. So I was easy prey.

It was hell at school, and the weekends were so boring I thought I'd die.

All in all, life was awful.

I came to the playing fields. Some lads were kicking a football around in the mist.

There were only three other people watching, and a dog. The players were rubbish. They couldn't even pass the ball, and both teams missed open goals. There was a lot of swearing and fouling, too.

And they call it the Beautiful Game!

I got bored after five minutes and wandered away.

There was a big field of cabbages at the edge of town, and then a small wood. I decided to explore.

I set off along the path at the side of the cabbage field. Before I got to the wood, I heard the sound of an engine behind me.

I wanted to run, or hide. But there was nowhere to run to, and nowhere to hide.

You see, I knew who the motorbike belonged to.

Ross Davis was the school bully. He was big and spotty and ginger-haired, and he had a cruel, ugly mouth like a monkey's backside.

He had a new Suzuki trail bike, and he wanted everyone to know about it.

He was standing up on his bike, revving towards me. He skidded to a halt.

I couldn't move. I was scared stiff.

"If it isn't Danny the Fanny!" he said. He pulled off his helmet and stared at me.

My name is Danny Fanshaw. I suppose it was only a matter of time before someone like Ross gave me a nickname.

"Nice bike, Ross," I said.

"What do you know about bikes, Fanny?" he said.

I stood there like a statue, staring at his big, mud-covered boots. I couldn't bring myself to look him in the eye. I just waited for him to climb off his bike and hit me. What else could I do? If I ran, he'd come after me on his bike.

But instead of hitting me, Ross said, "Want to see something, Fanny?"

I stared at him. "What?"

"Follow me."

He jumped off his bike and pushed it along the path. I followed him. I thought he was going to take me into the wood, where no-one could see, and beat me up.

But we took the path around the wood. At last he stopped and pointed. "Look."

In a field next to the wood was a massive bonfire. It was 30 feet high, built from old floorboards, sofas and chairs and broken doors. It was all ready for Guy Fawkes' night, next week.

"What do you think?" he asked me.

I thought it was his bonfire. "It's great," I said.

"Great?" he sneered. "It's crap."

He pulled something from the pocket of his leather jacket and rattled it in front of my face.

It was a box of matches.

"One match," he said. "One match is all it'd take!"

6

Chapter 2
Up in Flames

Fire ...

It's a wonderful thing, fire. The world changed when humans discovered fire.

My world changed when I discovered fire.

Now Ross said, "One match, Fanny. Or maybe two or three."

He was grinning. "I've got some petrol." He pointed to the saddlebag behind his bike. "I'll soak the wood with it and you light the match, OK? Then we'll watch it go up in smoke!"

What made me do it? Maybe I was scared of Ross. If I didn't agree to do it, he'd beat me up.

But, to be honest, a part of me wanted to see the bonfire go up in flames. I was bored, and feeling low, and I wanted excitement. A thrill.

What did it matter that a lot of people were looking forward to Guy Fawkes' night? What did it matter that they'd worked hard to build the bonfire? I didn't think about any of that at the time. All I thought about was the excitement of watching it burn.

Ross could see that I was tempted. He laughed. "You up for it, Fanny Boy?"

I nodded.

"Great!" he said. He laid his bike on the ground and pulled a red, plastic can from the saddlebag.

He gave me the box of matches. I looked up and down the path. It was getting dark. There was no-one around.

We ran through the field towards the bonfire. Ross unscrewed the cap of the petrol can and danced around the bonfire like a lunatic. The petrol glugged from the can and filled the air with its wonderful smell.

Then Ross stood back. He was breathing hard. "There," he said. "Now it's your turn."

Now that the time had come to light the fire, I was scared. What if someone had seen us? What if someone had recognised me?

"Go on, then! Or are you chicken?"

I opened the box and took out a match.
I stepped closer to the bonfire. The smell of
petrol was so strong that I felt dizzy.

My heart was thumping.

I had been bored, right? I wanted
excitement.

Well, I thought, *this is excitement* ...

I knelt down and struck the match.
I shielded the dancing flame in my cupped
palm and moved it towards an old door which
glistened with petrol.

I threw the match and moved back quickly.

WHUMPH!

It's the most beautiful sound in the world.
It's partly a roar, partly a greedy breath — the
sound that a fairytale dragon might make.

We laughed and stepped back. The flame raced around the bonfire, spitting and crackling.

We ran off. Ross climbed onto his motorbike and roared off into the night.

But I wanted to see more. I mean, what's the point of lighting a fire and then running away? I wanted to watch it burn. I wanted the thrill of seeing what I'd done.

I ran into the wood and jumped behind a fallen tree trunk. I was safe there. No-one could see me, but I could see the fire.

At first, I thought it'd gone out. I thought that the petrol had burned away, and that the bonfire was too damp to burn.

Then, slowly, the flames took hold. The wood glowed and burst into flame. Soon the big pile of old doors and chairs was a raging inferno. I could feel the heat from this distance. The roar filled my ears like music.

I felt the blood pounding through my veins, and excitement exploding in my chest.

Then it got even better.

It was hard to believe that it could get better. What could be better than watching a fire that you had lit all by yourself?

I'll tell you. It got better when the people arrived.

At first it was a few men and women from the houses across the field. Then a load of kids turned up.

Everyone was staring around in the dark, trying to see who might have done this to their bonfire.

Then a police car arrived, and I nearly wet myself.

Five minutes later there was a big crowd of people standing around the bonfire. I counted a hundred men and women and kids, then lost count.

And I felt great. For the first time in my life I had done something that people had noticed. For the first time, I had made something happen! I was someone at last.

I was no longer being bullied, or being told to eat in my room. People weren't ignoring me, or thinking that I was a little runt.

A hundred people were watching *my* fire. I felt like an artist, or a performer on stage.

For the first time in my life, I felt I had real power.

When another police car arrived, and a copper climbed out and headed towards the wood, I took off. I ran through the trees. I was so excited that I wanted to yell and scream.

One match ...

I had discovered fire.

Chapter 3
Toilet Torture

I thought that things might be better at school after that. I thought that perhaps Ross might stop bullying me. After all, we had set fire to the bonfire together.

But I was wrong. Things didn't get better. They got a lot worse.

At breaktime I saw Ross with a bunch of his mates. They were smoking by the school kitchen.

I waved and walked across to them. I was nervous, I can tell you.

Sandra Robinson was with them, laughing and joking. She was the most beautiful girl in the world. She was 16, a year older than me. Tall and slim, with long, blonde hair that went all the way down to her bottom. Have you seen *The Lord of the Rings*? Well, Sandra was just like Galadriel, the Elven Queen.

But why was she hanging around with Ross and his gang of ugly thugs?

"Hi, Ross," I said. "Great on Saturday, wasn't it?"

He just stared at me. His lips tightened, so that his mouth looked all the more like a monkey's backside.

I went on, like a fool, "You should have stayed around. You should have seen all the fuss!"

Sandra was looking at me, cool. She took a long drag on her cigarette. She looked like a filmstar. I felt myself going red.

One of Ross's mates said, "What were you doing with Fanny, Ross?"

Everyone burst out laughing. Even Sandra smiled a little.

"That does it," Ross said. His big, stupid face was bright red with anger.

Before I knew it, he dived at me. He got my head in an armlock and squeezed. I cried out in pain.

I struggled, but I couldn't get away. Ross was bigger than me, and stronger. I was bent in two. It was all I could do to keep on my feet.

His mates were shouting, telling him what to do with me. "Hammer the little twat!"

"Kick his face in!"

"Shove his ugly head down the loo!"

Then Sandra said, "Leave him alone."

Did she really say that, or was I hearing things?

Anyway, Ross didn't listen to her. He dragged me around the corner towards the old outside toilets.

I knew what he was going to do. I struggled even more, but Ross just tightened his grip on my neck. I was choking. I couldn't breathe.

He kicked open the rotting door and dragged me into the toilet. Then he shut the door behind him, so his mates couldn't hear what he said.

He let go of me and punched me in the belly. I screamed and fell back against the wall. I slid to the ground, clutching my stomach.

Ross stood over me. "Listen, Fanny. If you ever breathe a word to anyone about Saturday night – if you tell a single soul – I'll break every bone in your pathetic, little body, right?"

I nodded. "OK! OK, Ross!"

"I was nowhere near the wood on Saturday night, right?" Ross said. "I never saw you or anyone then. You lit the bonfire all by yourself, OK?"

"OK!" I said.

"And another thing, don't come bugging me and my mates again."

"OK."

He kicked me in the belly. "I didn't hear you, Fanny! Speak up."

"OK!" I cried.

"And so you don't forget, I'll give you something to remember." He dragged me towards a toilet bowl. I cried out and struggled, but that just made it worse.

He punched me in the face, then thrust my head right down the loo. It stank of old piss and shit. At last, he let go of me, kicked me in the backside as a farewell, and walked away.

OK, I'll be honest. I was crying by then. My nose was bleeding and my head was bruised and I smelled of shit. On my hands and knees, I crawled out of the cubicle and fell against the wall, sobbing.

I heard the bell go for the end of break, but I was in so much pain that I couldn't move. *To hell with lessons*, I thought.

I'd wait a while, an hour or so, and then go home and get cleaned up.

But the thought of coming back to school tomorrow made me feel sick.

Then the toilet door opened, and I cried out in fright. I thought it was Ross coming back to hit me again, or one of his mates.

Chapter 4

An Angel

Winter sunlight flooded in and, for a second, I couldn't see the figure standing in the doorway.

Then she stepped forward and knelt in front of me.

It was Sandra Robinson. She looked like an angel. The sunlight made her hair glow.

She was gazing at me without smiling. She had that kind of face. Cool, superior.

She knew she was beautiful. She didn't have to smile to make herself look any better.

"Look at you, Danny Boy," she said. "Just look what he did to you."

"He's an animal!" I spat, sniffing back my tears.

"Ross is a swine," Sandra said. "Why don't you keep away from him?"

"I didn't think he'd go mad," I said, "after Saturday. I thought he might be OK."

She looked at me. "What did you two get up to on Saturday, then?"

"Nothing, just mucked around."

She pulled a crumpled tissue from her blazer pocket. "Here, clean yourself up. You've got ... *yuck* ... on your forehead."

"Thanks." I took the tissue and wiped my face.

She was shaking her head at me.
"Why can't you stick up for yourself, Danny?
I've seen him pick on you ever since you got
here. Someone's got to teach Ross a lesson."

I stared at her. "You don't like him?"

"Who? Ross? He's a pig!"

"So why do you hang round with him,
then?"

"Some of his mates are OK," she said.

I shrugged. "Well, I won't be teaching him
a lesson. I mean – look at me – I'm half his
size."

She smiled. "Size isn't everything," she
said. "What matters is what's in here."
And she touched her chest.

I stared at the gap between the buttons of her blouse. I could see the edge of her bra, white and lacy.

I went red.

Sandra smiled and stood up, and her legs seemed to go on forever. As she was leaving the toilets, she said, "And don't listen to what they say. You aren't ugly at all, Danny Boy."

I bunked off school for the rest of the day and went to the wood by the playing fields. I thought about what Sandra had said, and dreamed that she was my girlfriend.

How pathetic can you get? As if a girl like Sandra Robinson would look twice at a midget like me!

At four, I made my way home. Dad was at work, but Mum was in the kitchen with her glass of sherry.

"What on earth happened to your face?" she said. "Have you been bullied again?"

"Nah," I said. I didn't want Mum complaining to the Head. That'd only make things worse. "I did it playing footie."

But she went on and on, "Your brother Billy didn't stand for kids bullying him when he was at school, you know. He fought back. And look at him now."

I sighed. It was always Billy this, Billy that. Billy was my older brother. He was 22 now, a sergeant in the army. I was a big disappointment to my mum and dad. I was bad at school, bad at sports, and I was bullied.

Mum seemed to think it was all my fault that I was picked on. But what could I do about it?

Later I was watching TV in the front room with Mum and Dad. The sound of a motorbike engine droned on and on in the lane outside.

"It's that Davis lout again," Dad said.

I went to the window and peered through the curtains. Ross had stopped outside the house. He was sitting on his motorbike and smoking a fag. When he saw me looking, he lifted a hand and gave me the finger.

Then he raced off down the lane.

"Somebody ought to fix him and that bike of his," Dad said.

That night I lay in bed and stared at the ceiling. I remembered what Dad had said.

Somebody ought to fix Ross Davis and that bike of his ...

That's when I got the idea.

I knew how to fix Ross and his bike.

I was so excited that I couldn't get to sleep.

Chapter 5

The Greatest Day
of My Life!

I slipped out of bed, got dressed and went downstairs. I sat in the kitchen for a while and thought about what I was going to do. It was two o'clock in the morning. There would be no-one about at this time. Ross Davis lived down the lane, two minutes away.

I took a box of matches from where Mum kept them by the cooker. Then I had a thought. I went into the front room, picked up an old newspaper and stuffed it up my jacket.

Then I went back to the kitchen and got Dad's torch from the cupboard. I took the key from its hook, unlocked the back door, and slipped out. I locked the door behind me and hurried down the path and into the lane.

I was so excited I thought I was going to explode. But I was scared as well. I'd never done anything like this before – the bonfire was different. That time, when I'd left the house I hadn't known what I was going to do.

This time, I knew what I was going to do.

The lane was in darkness. There were no street-lamps to light my way, only a few stars. It was bitter cold and silent. It felt as if the whole world was asleep.

Ross Davis lived with his mum and dad and sister in a tumbledown farmhouse. His dad owned an old chicken farm – you could smell it a mile off.

I reached the dry-stone wall round Ross's yard and stopped.

Ross kept his motorbike in an old wooden hut. I had seen him lock it up one day. I had always thought that it wasn't a very safe place to keep a new bike – the planks of wood at the back of the hut were rotten and split.

I looked at the farmhouse. There were no lights on in any of the windows.

My heart was beating like a bongo drum as I climbed over the wall and ran towards the hut. I crouched behind it and got my breath back.

I was shaking with the thought of what I was going to do. But I couldn't turn back now. I remembered what Ross had done to me that day, in the toilet. I wanted revenge.

I pulled the torch from my pocket and shone it at the back of the hut. It seemed so bright that anyone passing down the lane might see it. But who would be passing at this time in the morning?

I saw a broken plank of wood. I reached out and tugged at it. The timber split with a sound like a strangled hen. I swore and switched off the torch.

I waited for ages, but there was no sound from the farmhouse.

So I tugged again, and this time the wood came away in my hand. I switched on the torch and looked at the hole. It wasn't big enough for me to crawl through, but it was a start. I pulled at the plank of wood next to it, and it came away easily.

Now there was a gap wide enough for me to get through.

I wormed my way through the hole, stood up and shone the torch around the hut.

And there was Ross Davis's brand-new motorbike, shining red and silver in the beam of light. It looked so new that it seemed a shame to destroy it.

This was the moment. I could walk away now, go home and forget about burning the bike.

But I wanted revenge. I wanted to hurt Ross Davis, just like he had hurt me.

And I wanted the thrill of setting fire to something. I wanted to watch the motorbike and the hut go up in roaring flames.

I unfastened the saddlebag at the back of the bike. The red petrol can was still there, but there wasn't much petrol left in it. Just enough to do what I wanted to do.

I took the newspaper from under my jacket, scrunched up the pages into balls, and stuffed them all over the motorbike – under the seat, in the spokes of the wheels, around the handlebars.

I took the lid off the can and shook the petrol all over the bike and the paper. I poured petrol in a big puddle all around the bike, and then dribbled some across the floor towards the gap in the wall.

Then I crawled through the hole and knelt down outside the shed. I switched off the torch. In the sudden darkness and silence I could hear my heart beating loudly.

I pulled the box of matches from my pocket. I slid open the box and took out a match.

One match … It was incredible that one match could be so powerful.

I held the match in shaking fingers. Then I struck it against the side of the box.

The flame seemed very bright in the dark night. I leaned forward and dropped the match through the gap in the hut.

Nothing happened. It went out before it hit the floor.

I looked around, but I was alone.

I was even more scared now. Perhaps I should just forget all about it, go home …

But I wanted to see the hut go up in a blaze of glory.

I struck another match, cupped it from the wind until it was burning strongly, then tossed it into the hut.

WHUMPH!

Again there was that beautiful, terrible sound – and the night was bright with fire. It was so bright that it blinded me. The heat pushed me back. I stumbled away and covered my eyes with my arm.

I ran to the wall, climbed over and stared at the hut.

As I watched, the back of the hut collapsed. I could see inside. The motorbike was covered with leaping, dancing flames. I almost shouted out with joy.

Then a light in the farmhouse went on, and I ran.

I didn't stop until I reached home.

In my room, I danced around and punched the air. *This*, I thought, *is the greatest day of my life!*

Chapter 6
You Did It!

For the first time in ages, I was looking forward to going to school.

I wanted to see what kind of mood Ross was in this morning. Would he be quiet, bad-tempered? Maybe he wouldn't even be at school. Maybe he would be in his room, roaring his eyes out at the loss of his motorbike.

In the yard before we went into class, Sandra Robinson came up to me. She looked worried.

"Danny, I'd bunk off if I were you!"

"What's up?" I asked. I felt sick.

"I dunno. Ross has lost his rag. He's wild. Says he's gonna kill you."

I smiled weakly. "What have I done?" I asked.

Sandra just shrugged. "Dunno. Look, I'd better go. If he sees me with you ..."

She hurried off, and I felt great that she'd warned me. But at the same time I was scared.

Maybe Ross was so angry at losing his bike that he wanted to take it out on me.

He couldn't possibly know that I had started the fire, could he?

Before I could even think about bunking off, the bell went and the teacher on duty saw me and said, "Hurry up, Fanshaw. In you go. Quick march!"

All through double English that morning, Ross glared at me.

At one point, he made a fist and smacked it into the palm of his hand.

I knew what I was going to do. As soon as the bell went, I would race out of the classroom before he could get me. I'd bunk off and spend the rest of the day in the wood.

But what about tomorrow, and the day after that? I couldn't bunk off school every day, could I?

I decided not to think about that. Anything could happen before tomorrow.

The lesson seemed to go on for ever. At last the teacher said, "OK, now pack up your books and sit still until – "

The bell rang, and I raced for the door.

I sprinted down the corridor, through the cloakroom and out of the swing doors. I was in the yard now and running for my life when I heard the door crash open behind me.

Then I made a big mistake. I looked over my shoulder. Ross and his mates piled through the door, chasing after me.

And then I tripped up and fell flat on my face.

The first kick landed in my belly, winding me. The next kick nearly broke my leg.

After that, I lost count of the number of kicks and punches that seemed to hit me out of the blue.

Ross picked me up, got my head in an armlock, and marched me across the playground. "You know where you're going, don't you, Fanny Boy?"

He pushed me into the toilet block and closed the door behind him. I could hear his mates outside.

"Smash the little ratbag!"

"Drown him in the loo!"

Ross pushed me against the wall and stared at me.

I'd never seen him look so angry. "It was you, wasn't it? You did it!"

"Did what?" I cried.

"You know what, you little scumball. You burned my bike!"

"Don't know what you're talking about!" I yelled.

He kicked me. It was so quick and nasty and painful that I burst out crying. I'd never been as frightened in all my life.

"Admit it, Fanny. You burned down the shed, didn't you?"

"I swear ... I swear, I didn't do anything. Honest, Ross."

He punched me in the mouth. The pain seemed to fill my head. I tasted blood on my lip.

"I'm going to make your life a misery, Fanny. Understand? I'm gonna beat you senseless every day until you confess. You'll wish you'd never been born!"

"Ross, I swear ... Honest, I never did – "

He punched me again, then dragged me into the toilet cubicle. I cried out, but it made no difference. He forced my head down into the loo.

When I thought it was all over, he gave me one last kick in the backside. The top of my head hit the back of the toilet and I nearly passed out.

I heard him walk away and the door bang shut.

A long time after that I crawled out of the cubicle and lay on the floor. I hurt all over. My balls ached where he'd kicked me. My head throbbed. I could taste blood in my mouth. My lips felt as thick as bits of liver.

And I had this to look forward to every school day from now on ...

"Oh, Danny Boy."

I thought I was hearing things.

I opened my eyes and looked up.

An angel was staring down at me.

"I told you to bunk off, Danny Boy. Now look what's happened." Sandra took a tissue from her blazer pocket, wet it with her spit, and wiped my face.

It was painful and wonderful all at the same time.

"I wish I could help you," Sandra said.

I smiled. I didn't believe she was saying this. "Nothing you can do," I said. "Ross is a swine. He said he was going to beat me up every day ... "

Sandra pulled a face. "Ouch," she said. "I could say something to him, but he wouldn't take any notice. Why don't you see the Head?"

I tried to laugh. "As if that'd do anything! Ross would just get me after school, then."

I struggled to my feet. I felt dizzy.

"Where are you going?" she asked.

I shrugged. "Dunno, anywhere but back in there." I smiled at her. "Thanks, Sandra."

I staggered out of the toilet block and didn't look back. I heard her say, in a small voice, "Take care, Danny. OK?"

I walked home through the wood, taking my time. Slowly, the pain went away.

I thought about the future. I thought about going to school every day, and what Ross would do to me.

What could I do about it?

Then I had an idea. It was an idea so big and terrible that I didn't know if I could do it.

One match, I thought.

Chapter 7

The Big One!

That night I stayed awake until two in the morning. Then I climbed out of bed and got dressed. I was scared, I can tell you. I mean, setting fire to a bonfire and a hut was bad enough. But this was something very different. This was something much bigger.

This was the big one ...

And it was the only thing I could do to stop Ross bullying me.

Dad kept a can of petrol in the garage. I got the torch and matches from the kitchen and let myself out of the back door.

I took the can of petrol from the garage and set off.

What I was going to do tonight would make the news. It'd be in the local newspapers, and even on *Look North* and *Calendar*. That almost made me wonder if I should go through with it.

I even stopped walking and thought about it.

But there was no other way to stop Ross from bullying me. I *had* to do it.

The night was freezing cold and cloudless. A big, full moon stared down at me. There was no-one about. I cut through the playing fields and walked around the wood.

The school was a big, old building surrounded by sports fields. It looked different in the darkness – silent and almost spooky.

I hurried across the football pitch, towards the P.E. hall.

There was a window with a broken catch at the corner of the building. It was always swinging open when we were in the middle of P.E., freezing us.

I pushed open the window and climbed inside.

I stood in the darkness, listening.
The only thing I could hear was my breathing.
It felt strange to be in the P.E. hall in the middle of the night. Usually the place was noisy with kids. Now it was deadly quiet.

I was too frightened to turn on my torch, in case someone saw the light from outside.

After a minute or two, my eyes grew used to the darkness. I could see the five-a-side goal and the door at the far end of the hall.

I moved towards the door and pushed through, into the corridor. It was dark in there, so I switched on my torch.

I had it all planned. I knew exactly what I was going to do. I would pour petrol in every classroom, leaving a trail on the floor to make sure that the fire spread.

I hurried through the school, to the classrooms on the far side of the building. I slipped into the Maths room and stared around me.

"Goodbye, Maths," I said, and splashed petrol over the desks and chairs.

I moved to the next room and did the same there. The stench of petrol filled the air. I was starting to love the sour smell. It was magic, like matches.

I went from classroom to classroom, leaving a trail of petrol along the corridors. In each room, I made sure I poured petrol in every corner, over every surface that would burn.

"Goodbye, Science!" I said. "Goodbye, Geography!"

I came to the History room and laughed. Last week we had learned all about the Great Fire of London!

How about the Great Fire of Gresham Secondary School?

I splashed petrol all over and laughed like a fool.

Then I made my way back towards the P.E. hall, dribbling petrol along the floor behind me. When I got there, I still had about a cupful of petrol left. I could hear it splashing around in the bottom of the can.

I poured the last of the petrol on the floor, dribbling a trail towards the open window.

I climbed out and stood in the fresh, cold air. *This is it*, I told myself. *The Big One!*

I opened the matchbox. I almost dropped the matches, I was shaking so much. At last I fumbled out a match, took a deep breath, and struck it against the box.

Then I dropped it through the window.

Instantly the whole P.E. hall filled with orange flames. A great roar filled the air like a thousand raging dragons. The flames danced along the floor and through the door towards the classrooms. I stood back and watched through the windows as the flames raced along the length of the building. Soon, every classroom was bright with fire.

I was laughing as I ran.

I crossed the football fields and sprinted into the wood. I knelt down behind a tree and watched the fun.

In the distance, I could see the school as it burned down. Great flames licked up into the night, filling the air with a bright orange glow.

Ten minutes later, I heard the sound of a fire engine. It grew louder as it got nearer. I saw it pull into the schoolyard, and then a second truck and a third.

I felt like standing up and dancing with joy.   I was filled with a wonderful, bubbling excitement.

The tiny figures of the firemen raced around the building. They looked like ants from this distance. They sprayed water onto the burning building, but by this time, there was nothing they could do to save the school.

Soon, a crowd of people had gathered outside the school. There were even some older people in their nighties and dressing-gowns – they had all come out to watch the show. Then two police cars arrived.

I felt proud, I can tell you.

About an hour later, the crowd disappeared as everyone went back to bed. The school was just a burned-out skeleton in the moonlight. The fire engines were still there, with firemen spraying foam onto the smoking ruins.

No more school for a while! I thought as I made my way home.

Chapter 8

Going Out with Sandra

I was still asleep when Mum knocked on my door in the morning.

"What?" I said.

She poked her head around the door. "That was the school secretary on the phone," she said. "You won't be going in today, or for the rest of the week. The school burned down last night. It's on TV now."

I turned on my TV. I was just in time to see the last minute of the news report. It showed the school, blackened and roofless. Kids were dancing up and down in front of the camera.

I felt a strange sensation, then. I felt amazed that I had done this to the school. But I also felt a strange mixture of satisfaction and shame.

I mean, what I had done was wrong – but I had done it for a reason. I told myself that I was right to have done what I did. I mean, how else could I have stopped Ross from bullying me?

Then they interviewed the Head, old Mr Andrews.

He said that the school would be closed down for two weeks, probably more. They would be getting some Portacabin classrooms, but it would take time to put them up.

I thumped the air as if I'd scored a goal.

I was playing on my PlayStation 2 when Mum looked in again.

"Danny, there's a friend of yours downstairs. Hurry up."

A friend? But I had no friends in Barnsley.

I hurried down, wondering who it might be.

"Hi, Danny."

Sandra Robinson sat in the kitchen, sipping a cup of tea.

Mum said, "Sandra and me were talking about the school, weren't we?"

Sandra smiled. "Just think, two weeks off school, Danny."

I went red. I must have looked a right fool, standing there in the doorway with my mouth hanging open.

55

Sandra seemed to fill the kitchen with light.

I found my tongue. "Er ... hi, Sandra. Hey, want to see my new PlayStation 2?"

Sandra smiled. "If it's OK with you, Mrs Fanshaw."

Mum smiled. "Of course, go and enjoy yourselves."

I showed Sandra up the stairs. I still couldn't believe it. Sandra Robinson, come to see me? Perhaps I was still asleep, and this was a dream.

Sandra looked around my room. "Hey, this is cool," she said, "for a boy's room."

"Thanks," I murmured.

She sat on the bed. Her long hair reached down to the covers. She crossed her legs and smiled at me.

"Amazing about the school, isn't it?"

I nodded. "Amazing. Hey, want a game of *Airblade*?"

"Great."

For the next hour we played *Airblade*, and do you know something? I came to see Sandra Robinson as a human being. I mean, I was no longer scared of her. She was still beautiful, and I couldn't take my eyes off her, but she was funny and kind and ... well, for some reason she seemed to like me.

Amazing, I know.

It was almost two o'clock when she sighed and said, "Well, I've really got to be going. I'm meeting my mum in town."

I nodded. I didn't know what to say. I showed her downstairs.

"Hey, you doing anything tonight?" she asked at the front door.

I went red again. "No."

"Seen *Terminator 3*, Danny?"

I shook my head.

She smiled. "Why don't we go and see it together?"

I gulped. "That'd be ... that'd be great."

"OK. Meet you at seven outside the cinema. Bye, Danny!"

I said goodbye, then watched her walk away. My heart was beating so fast I thought it was going to burst.

"What a lovely young lady," Mum said when I went back inside.

I went up to my room, lay down and closed my eyes. But I could still see Sandra's beautiful smile in my mind.

Just a short while ago, my life had been hell.

Now, everything seemed a lot better.

Chapter 9
Gaz

I saw Sandra every day after that.
We went to see a film every night. I can't remember what we saw. All I can remember is Sandra, how she chatted and laughed.

She laughed at every joke I made! Me, the comedian! It made me feel great.

The first time she slipped her hand into mine made me feel great, too.

And the first kiss ...

We were walking back from the cinema, through the park.

Sandra stopped walking and tugged my hand.

"What?" I said.

"Here," she said. "Stand here."

She stood in front of me, staring into my eyes. "You ever kissed a girl?" she asked.

"Once," I lied.

Sandra kissed me, then smiled. "Was it as good as that?" she said.

I felt as if my face was burning. "No," I said.

She hugged me, and I have never felt as happy in my life. It was even better than watching buildings burn ...

"I don't understand," I said.

"What don't you understand?"

"Why you ... why – ?"

"Why do I think you're gorgeous?" she said. She laughed. "You're different, not like the others. They're always trying to prove themselves. Acting big. They're so immature! You're ... I don't know. Quiet, thoughtful. And you're funny. And a little bit good-looking, too ..."

I pulled her to me. "I think I love you, Sandra."

She laughed. "Just *think*?" she said.

That was the happiest day of my life. I should have known that things couldn't stay that good for long.

The trouble started the very next day.

I was walking over to Sandra's house when three lads blocked my way.

At first I thought they were mates of Ross – but they were older than him. They were about 18, and mean-looking. They wore baseball caps and nose studs.

Then I thought, *Maybe they fancy Sandra, and don't want me seeing her ...*

"How you doing, Danny?" one of them said.

I just looked at him. My heart was hammering. How did they know my name? "What do you want?" I said.

"Oh, nothing much. Just a quiet chat."

"I've got to go," I began.

One of the others stopped me. He placed a hand on my chest. "Not so fast, sunshine. Listen to what Gaz has to say, OK?"

I stared at the lad called Gaz. "What?" I said.

"It's like this, Danny," Gaz said. "We need your help, like."

I shook my head. "I don't understand."

"Then I'll explain," Gaz said. "You see, we know what you're good at."

My stomach flipped. I felt sick. "What?"

Gaz grinned. His teeth were bad. "You see," Gaz said, "we know who burned the school down."

I tried to get away, but the other two stopped me and pushed me against the wall. "Listen to what Gaz has to say to you!" one of them said.

Gaz smiled. "You did a good job, Danny. Very professional. Couldn't have done better myself."

"It wasn't me!" I yelled.

Gaz shoved his face very close to mine. "Listen, you little runt, I don't like liars. We know it was you because we saw you."

I just stared at him.

"Also," Gaz went on, "we have evidence."

"What evidence?" I asked.

Gaz nodded to one of the others. They passed him a rucksack, and Gaz lifted out a petrol can. He held it by its side, not by the handle.

It was the petrol can I had used to burn down the school. I must have left it outside the P.E. hall when I ran off.

I thought I was going to faint with fear.

"You did a good job, Danny. But not good enough. You left this behind at the scene of the crime. Not clever, Danny. Not clever at all."

"It doesn't belong to me – " I began.

"No? I wonder if the police would agree, if they found your fingerprints on the handle?"

I stared at him. "What do you want?"

"Your help," Gaz said. "Your co-operation. And if you don't agree to help us, we'll turn you in. Isn't that right, boys?"

They grinned and nodded. "Too right," they said.

"What do I have to do?"

Gaz smiled. "Good boy, Danny. I knew you'd see sense. We'll pick you up at midnight, OK? We'll be outside the park gates. And if you don't come ..." He lifted the petrol can and grinned horribly.

I made my way to Sandra's house in a daze. We went up to her room, lay on the bed and kissed.

She was as beautiful as ever, but I felt terrible. She lay beside me, staring into my eyes.

"Danny, is everything all right? You know, you can tell me."

I smiled, and kissed her. "Everything's fine," I lied.

I mean, I loved her, but how could I tell her the truth?

I tried to forget about Gaz and his mates, but it was impossible.

What did they want me to do tonight?

Chapter 10
In Deep

At ten to twelve that night I left the house and hurried to the park.

I'd thought about not turning up. But if Gaz and his mates did tell the police that they'd seen me at the school, and showed them the petrol can with my fingerprints on it, I'd be in big trouble.

They were waiting for me outside the park. They were huddled in a little group, smoking.

"Danny Boy!" Gaz said when I joined them. He slapped me on the shoulder. "Glad you could make it!"

"What do you want?" I asked.

"Get in the van," Gaz said.

He pointed to an old Volkswagen van parked at the side of the road. I found out later on that they'd stolen it.

Gaz drove, and I sat in the passenger seat. His mates were in the back.

"Where are we going?" I asked. I felt sick. They might be taking me anywhere.

"Just a couple of miles," one of the others said.

I said, "I'd like to know what you want me to do."

Gaz looked at me and grinned. "All in good time, Danny."

We took the main road away from town. There wasn't much traffic. Five minutes later, we turned off the road and entered an industrial estate. We drove past ugly factories and warehouses. Gaz slowed the car.

"Where are we going?" I asked.

"Almost there," one of the others said.

Gaz pulled into the side of the road. He nodded to one of his mates in the back, who lifted something up and passed it between the front seats.

It was a can of petrol.

I stared at it.

"Take it," Gaz said.

I took the heavy can and placed it between my feet. Then Gaz pulled something from his pocket and passed it to me. A box of matches.

"What do you want me to do?" I was sweating with fear.

Gaz pointed across the road to a big factory behind a high fence. Near the fence was a Portacabin.

"See that Portacabin, Danny?" Gaz said. "We want you to burn it down."

My stomach turned. I felt sick.

"Now this is what you do," Gaz went on. "There's a gap in the fence, just there. Get through the fence and crawl under the Portacabin. There's lots of old rubbish under there, newspapers and stuff that'll burn really well."

"You want me to set fire to the Portacabin?" I said.

"You're quick, Danny Boy. That's exactly what we want you to do. You're an expert, see?"

I stared at the Portacabin. "But there's a light on inside!" I said. "There might be someone in there!"

Gaz laughed. "Don't you worry. The security guard will be doing his rounds. He's just left the light on."

"What if someone sees me?" I said. I was shaking now. I thought I was going to be sick.

"It's up to you to make sure no-one does see you, Danny," Gaz said.

"Why do you want me to do this?"

One of the others in the back leaned forward and said, "The less you know, the better."

Gaz looked at his watch. "OK, let's get cracking. Danny, do your stuff."

What could I do? If I refused, they'd turn me in, or beat me up ...

I took a big breath and opened the van door. I hurried across the road with the petrol can in one hand and the box of matches in the other. I found the gap in the fence and stopped. I looked at the Portacabin. The light was still on, but I couldn't see anyone inside.

I looked back at the van. Gaz made an angry gesture for me to get on with it.

I got down on my hands and knees and crawled through the gap in the fence. Then I ran towards the Portacabin and ducked down when I reached it. My heart was thumping fast with fear.

I looked back across the road. Gaz and his mates were staring out at me. I got down on my hands and knees and crawled into the dark, smelly gap under the Portacabin.

Gaz was right. There were lots of old newspapers and cardboard and rubbish under there, and it was all dry. It would go up like a bomb.

I crawled to the far end of the building, stopped and unscrewed the lid of the can. The smell of the petrol made me feel dizzy, and I thought I was going to pass out.

I tipped up the can and poured the petrol everywhere. The smell was incredible. I covered the ground with petrol, all over the old papers and cardboard. Then I crawled backwards, the way I had come, and tipped out more petrol.

I backed out from under the building and crouched down. I slid open the box of matches and took one out.

Then I stopped.

I could hear something.

It was the sound of a radio, and it was coming from inside the Portacabin. Music.

Was there someone in there after all?

What could I do? I panicked. I wasn't thinking straight. I just wanted to be out of there.

But if I didn't do what Gaz wanted me to do, they'd tell the cops that I'd burned down the school ...

So I struck the match and tossed it under the Portacabin – and then I ran.

I heard a great *WHUMPH!* behind me, but I didn't look back. I squirmed through the fence and ran across the road.

But the van wasn't there.

Gaz and his mates had gone off without me.

I turned around.

The Portacabin was ablaze now. It was burning like a bonfire, and from inside I thought I could hear someone screaming ...

I took off. I ran like the wind. I didn't think, I just sprinted along the road. When I came to the main road, I turned left and ran.

****

Hours later, I arrived home. I let myself in the back door and crept up to my room.

All I wanted to do was to hold Sandra in my arms and cry like a baby.

But all I could see was the burning Portacabin and all I could hear was someone screaming inside ...

Chapter 11
A Bad Dream?

It was late when I woke up.

At first I thought that last night had been a bad dream. Then I smelled the petrol on my clothes, and I remembered the burning Portacabin, and the screams ...

It was a Friday, and Mum and Dad were at work. I turned on the TV and waited for the local news to come on.

I walked up and down the front room, thinking about what I had done last night, what a fool I had been.

Then I heard the sound of a motorbike outside. I looked through the window. Ross was riding up and down in the lane on his brand new Suzuki.

When he passed, he looked in through the window. I backed off so he couldn't see me.

There had been no school all week. Ross had had no chance to beat me up, so he had come looking for me ...

Why was life so awful? When would all the bad stuff stop happening to me?

I thought about going back to school, when the bullying would start all over again ...

Then the local news came on, and I forgot all about Ross.

If I thought things were bad before, now they were even worse.

I collapsed onto the floor and listened to the news report. There was a picture of the burned-out Portacabin, and a reporter was saying, "Another big fire. The Barnsley Arsonist has struck again ..."

I listened, and I could hardly believe what I heard.

The reporter said that thieves had burned down a Portacabin last night. While security guards had tried to put out the fire, the thieves had broken into the factory and stolen 100,000 pounds' worth of computers.

So that was why Gaz and his mates had wanted me to set fire to the Portacabin ...

But that was not all.

There was worse to come.

The reporter went on to say that Arthur Barnes, 59, a security guard, had been in the Portacabin when it was set alight. He had survived, but had been badly burned.

The reporter said that he would be scarred for life.

I turned off the TV. I was too shocked to do anything. I just stared at the wall. I couldn't even cry.

The security guard would be scarred for life ...

And it was all my fault.

I just sat there for a long, long time. Then I decided what to do.

I rang Sandra's mobile phone and asked her to come over to my place.

"What is it, Danny? Are you OK?"

I said I was fine. "I just want to tell you something."

She said, "You want to finish with me, don't you? You're tired of me!"

"Sandra, of course not. It's nothing like that. I love you. But I need to talk."

She said that she'd be right over.

I sat in the front room, listening to the drone of Ross's motorbike outside, and thought about what I was going to tell Sandra.

Chapter 12

Confession Time

Sandra arrived ten minutes later.

"Danny!" She hugged me. "Something's wrong. I can tell by your face. What's happened?"

She was worried, and yet I thought that she had never looked so beautiful.

I took her to my room and we sat on the bed.

This was going to be the hardest thing I had ever done, but I had to tell her.

"Danny – what is it?"

I took her hand. "I've got to tell you this. I hope you won't hate me, but I've got to tell someone. I can't keep it from you."

So I began at the beginning. I told her about last Saturday, when Ross and me had set fire to the bonfire. Then I told her about how Ross had bullied me so that I wouldn't tell anyone about the bonfire.

I told her that he had made my life hell.

"I had an idea, Sandra. I couldn't face school. I thought that if school wasn't there, if I didn't have to go, then Ross wouldn't be able to beat me up."

She just sat there on the bed, staring at me with her massive eyes. At last she said,

84

"You ... it was you who burned the school down, wasn't it?"

I nodded. I couldn't bring myself to look at her.

The silence seemed to go on for ever.

Then she reached out a hand and squeezed my fingers. "I understand, Danny. I still love you. I won't tell anyone."

I almost cried then. I shook my head. "That isn't all," I said. "It gets worse ..."

"Danny?"

I took a deep breath and told her about Gaz and his mates, and how they had made me light the fire under the Portacabin.

"It was my fault, Sandra. I shouldn't have done it. I should have been stronger and said no."

She squeezed my fingers even harder. "But the police might not find out," she said.

"I think they will," I told her. "I think they'll start a big investigation. It'll only be a matter of time before they find that it was Gaz who stole the computers. And he'll tell them that it was me who lit the fire."

I stopped, then said, "There was a security guard in the Portacabin, Sandra. He was badly burned in the fire."

I looked up. Sandra was weeping. Big, silver tears rolled down her cheeks. Her hand gripped my fingers, hard. "Danny, you aren't a bad person. You've done bad things, but you aren't bad."

"The police won't think that," I said.

"But they might not find out!"

I stared at her for a long time. "Sandra, I want you to do something for me."

"What? Tell me ..."

"I've been thinking about the future. About my life. I mean, when the school's repaired, things will be just as bad. Ross will make my life a misery. I can't go through all that again."

"What are you going to do, Danny?" Sandra said, and she looked frightened.

I looked at her. My heart was beating so fast I thought I was going to pass out. "Will you phone the police and tell them that you know who started all the fires? Will you tell them to come here?"

She wept. "I can't, Danny! I can't do that to you!"

"It's the only way," I said. "I've got to tell them. They'll find out, sooner or later.

And, don't you see, if they lock me up, then Ross won't be able to get at me."

"And I'll tell them why you did it," Sandra said. "How Ross bullied you."

She held me and cried for what seemed like a long time.

Then she took her mobile phone from her bag and dialled 999.

Chapter 13
The End

Two coppers arrived ten minutes later.

It was like something from *The Bill*. They questioned me about the fires and I told them everything. I expected them to be hard, but they even smiled, and sounded apologetic when they said that they would have to take me down to the station.

They asked where my parents were, and I told them where they worked.

As we were about to go, Sandra said, "I want to come with him!"

One of the coppers said, "I'm afraid that's not possible, love. He'll be home in a bit. You'll be able to see him then, OK?"

I held Sandra for a long time. One of the policemen stayed in the house and phoned my mum and dad, and the other led me outside.

He marched me along the lane, and pushed me into the back of the waiting police car.

I looked through the back window. Sandra was standing outside the house, looking so lonely. The car set off, and I waved to her.

She lifted a hand and waved back, sadly.

I saw Ross Davis. He was sitting on his motorbike in the lane and staring at me, his mouth open wide. I turned and looked at him through the back window.

Then I laughed and gave him the finger.

Barrington Stoke would like to thank all its readers for commenting on the manuscript before publication and in particular:

Caroline Beaton
Rebecca Bryers
Rebecca Burleigh
Catriona Campbell
Christianna Campbell
Kevin Clark
Catherine Cover
Tony Dickson
Adrian Gauhl
Michelle Gibson
Sharmeen Gordji
Jane Hodgkinson
Kristel King
Danielle Main
Leta McEwan
Kelly McGuinness
Alex Rae
G. Shaw-Howells
Nicola Claire Sleigh
Kirsty Smillie
Miss B. Spurgin
Robyn Warburton

Become a Consultant!

Would you like to give us feedback on our titles before they are published? Contact us at the address below – we'd love to hear from you!

Barrington Stoke, 10 Belford Terrace, Edinburgh, EH4 3DQ
Tel: 0131 315 4933 Fax: 0131 315 4934
E-mail: info@barringtonstoke.co.uk
Website: www.barringtonstoke.co.uk

More Teen Titles!

Joe's Story by Rachel Anderson 1-902260-70-8
Playing Against the Odds by Bernard Ashley 1-902260-69-4
Harpies by David Belbin 1-842990-31-4
TWOCKING by Eric Brown 1-842990-42-X
To Be A Millionaire by Yvonne Coppard 1-902260-58-9
All We Know of Heaven by Peter Crowther 1-842990-32-2
The Ring of Truth by Alan Durant 1-842990-33-0
Falling Awake by Viv French 1-902260-54-6
The Wedding Present by Adèle Geras 1-902260-77-5
The Cold Heart of Summer by Alan Gibbons 1-842990-80-2
Shadow on the Stairs by Ann Halam 1-902260-57-0
Alien Deeps by Douglas Hill 1-902260-55-4
Partners in Crime by Nigel Hinton 1-842991-02-7
The New Girl by Mary Hooper 1-842991-01-9
Dade County's Big Summer by Lesley Howarth 1-842990-43-8
Runaway Teacher by Pete Johnson 1-902260-59-7
No Stone Unturned by Brian Keaney 1-842990-34-9
Wings by James Lovegrove 1-842990-11-X
A Kind of Magic by Catherine MacPhail 1-842990-10-1
Stalker by Anthony Masters 1-842990-81-0
Clone Zone by Jonathan Meres 1-842990-09-8
The Dogs by Mark Morris 1-902260-76-7
Turnaround by Alison Prince 1-842990-44-6
Dream On by Bali Rai 1-842990-45-4
All Change by Rosie Rushton 1-902260-75-9
Fall Out by Rosie Rushton 1-842990-74-8
The Blessed and The Damned by Sara Sheridan 1-842990-08-X
Double Vision by Norman Silver 1-842991-00-0